The Berenstain Bears
COUNT THEIR
BLESSINGS

Small bears get big eyes
when they take off and roam,
and sometimes forget
all the good stuff at home.

A First Time Book®

BLESSINGS

Stan & Jan Berenstain

Random House New York

Copyright © 1995 by Berenstain Enterprises, Inc. All rights reserved under International and Pan-American Copyright Conventions. Published in the United States by Random House, Inc., New York, and simultaneously in Canada by Random House of Canada Limited, Toronto.

Library of Congress Cataloging-in-Publication Data:
Berenstain, Stan.   The Berenstain Bears count their blessings / Stan & Jan Berenstain.   p.   cm. — (First time books)   SUMMARY: During a frightful thunderstorm, Brother and Sister Bear learn that Mama and Papa's love and protection are better blessings than more Bearbie dolls and video games.
ISBN: 0-679-87707-X (pbk.) — 0-679-97707-4 (lib. bdg.)
[1. Bears—Fiction.   2. Thunderstorms—Fiction.   3. Family Life—Fiction.]
I. Berenstain, Jan.   II. Title.   III. Series: Berenstain, Stan. First time books.
PZ7.B4483Bec   1995   [E]—dc20   95-1629

Manufactured in the United States of America   20 19

"Mama," said Sister Bear one
day after school, "may I go over
to Lizzy's house to play this
afternoon?"

"Yes, you may," said Mama Bear.
"But be sure not to leave a mess for
Lizzy's mom, and be sure to be
home in time for supper."

As Mama watched Sister skipping happily over the hill to Lizzy's house, she sighed. She knew exactly what was going to happen when Sister got home. And it wasn't just when she got home from Lizzy's. It was the same thing when she got home from Anna's, or Queenie's.

"Anna's got her own phone in her room!" Sister would complain. Or, "Queenie's got her own phone *and* her own TV in her room!" But Lizzy's was the worst. That was because Lizzy had the biggest collection of Bearbie dolls, ever.

"But you have a Bearbie doll," Mama would say. "And your Bearbie has lovely clothes."

"But Lizzy has *lots* of Bearbies!" complained Sister. "She's got High Fashion Bearbie, Supersport Bearbie, Tropical Bearbie, Motorcycle Bearbie, and Just Married Bearbie—and Just Married Bearbie has a whole trousseau!"

Then Mama usually said, "Please, Sister! I've heard quite enough about Lizzy's Bearbie collection!"

It wasn't much better with Brother Bear. Of course, it wasn't Bearbie dolls with Brother. It was video games for his Game Bear player. When Brother came home from Cousin Freddy's house, it was "You ought to see how many video games Freddy has! He's got Space Avenger, Rocket Rangers, Killer Koyote…" and on and on and on.

Mama looked around. Where *was* Brother? She asked Papa Bear when he came in from his shop for a tea break.

"Brother asked if he could go over to Cousin Fred's," he said. "I told him, sure. He'll be back in time for supper." There was a distant rumble of thunder. "Hmm," he added. "There must be a storm coming."

That's right, thought Mama.
With Sister at Lizzy's and
Brother at Fred's, there was
bound to be a storm coming—
a storm of complaints about
how many Bearbies Lizzy had
and how many video games
Fred had. Mama got upset just
thinking about it. But as the
thunder got louder and the
storm came closer, she
began to worry.

She was about to call to have the cubs sent home when she heard them coming up the front steps. They came in the door just ahead of the rain. It didn't take long for the complaining to start.

"Lizzy just got *Equestrienne* Bearbie!" said Sister. "It's brand-new! It comes with riding clothes and a beautiful horse!"

"You think *that's* something?" cried Brother. "Cousin Fred's got three new video games! Three!"

"Now look, you two!" said Mama. "I've heard quite enough about what you *don't* have. It would be very nice if you would start appreciating the things you *do* have. It's called 'counting your blessings.'"

Just then, there was a big streak of lightning, followed by a big clap of thunder, and the rain started coming down very hard. The cubs weren't exactly afraid of lightning and thunder, but this looked as if it was going to be a really big storm, and they were a little nervous.

"Well," said Mama, "like this warm, cozy house that protects us against the weather. That's one blessing." Now it was really pouring. The wind was whipping the curtains and blowing rain into the house. Mama and Papa rushed about, closing windows.

There was another lightning
flash and another thunderclap.

CRRRAACK!!!

"And we have each other," said Mama, bringing the cubs close. "That's another blessing." That's when the biggest lightning flash yet lit up the sky. It was followed by a clap of thunder that shook the very air.

KABO

"Yipe!" cried Sister,
jumping into Mama's arms.
"Help!" cried Brother,
jumping into Papa's arms.

"And you've got a mama and papa who love you," said Mama. The lights started to flicker. Then, after a few flickers, they went out.

"And you have a papa who knows how to make a fire in the fireplace," said Papa. Soon he had a cheery fire roaring.

"And a mama who knows how to make cocoa over it," said Mama. She hung a cook pot over the fire. Soon they were sitting in the glow of the fire, sipping hot, sweet cocoa. Mmm! What a blessing that was!

The storm kept getting worse. The lightning flashed brighter and brighter.

BOOO

The thunder crashed louder and louder.

"Th-th-that last flash seemed awful close," said Sister.

"Nothing to worry about," said Papa. "It was at least five thousand feet away."

"How can you tell?" asked Brother.

"Easy," said Papa. "You see, sound travels a lot slower than light. So when you see the flash, start counting the seconds—one…two…three…—until you hear the thunder. Then you figure about a thousand feet for each second." Just then there was a flash.

The cubs started counting.

"One...two...three..." On "four" there was a big thunderclap.

"That flash was about four thousand feet away!" said Sister.

"Very good!" said Papa.

BOOOOMM

Outside, the storm raged on.

But inside their sturdy tree house, the Bear family was cozy and warm. As the storm grew worse, they sipped cocoa and counted out the thunder. The counting helped. Papa explained what lightning and thunder were. Lightning was a big electrical flash that traveled between storm clouds and burned up the air. Thunder was the sound of air rushing in to the burnt space. That helped too.

Gradually the storm
eased. The rain slowed
and stopped, and the
lights came back on. The
Bear family sighed a big
sigh of relief.

Then Sister started counting again.
"Why are you counting, dear?" asked
Mama. "The storm is over."
"I'm doing what you
said, Mama," she
said. "I'm counting
my blessings."

So while Papa set the table
and Mama started supper,
Sister went upstairs to play
with her Bearbie doll, and
Brother tried to reach the next
level on one of his video
games.

"You know, my dear," said Papa. "There are birthdays and Christmas coming. Do you have any ideas for the cubs?"

"I thought perhaps a Just Married Bearbie for Sister and a couple of video games for Brother might be nice," Mama said. "What do you think?"

"I think we should count *our* blessings too," said Papa.